This book belongs to;_____

From;_____

For my grandchildren Cedric, Illianna, Ashton and Conner.

Wilber's Scary Day!
Copyrights © 2017 story and illustration by Collette Dahl Lorentzen
All rights reserved.

First edition - 04/2017

Wilber's Scary Day!

Written & Illustrated
by
Collette Dahl
Lorentzen

Wilber is a happy puppy that loves to play. He likes to roll in the green grass and play in the water puddles when it rains.

Wilber smells everything and anything. That's what puppies do best! Wilber has a little boy, Oliver, and they do almost everything together.

But sometimes Wilber's nose gets him into trouble and takes him places he should not go.

One day Wilber was just having fun, running through the grass, jumping, smelling the flowers, and barking at all sorts of bugs and things.

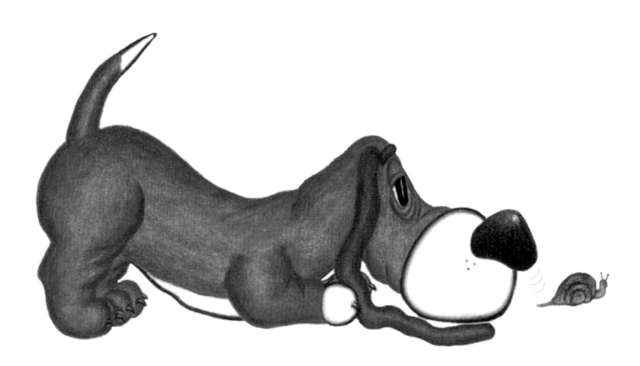

Jost then, a beautiful butterfly landed on Wilber's nose for a brief moment.

This made Wilber very curious, so he followed the butterfly as he flew all around the bushes and the flowers.

This butterfly found a butterfly friend. The two of them flew all over, on flowers, across the stream, and into the dark forest.

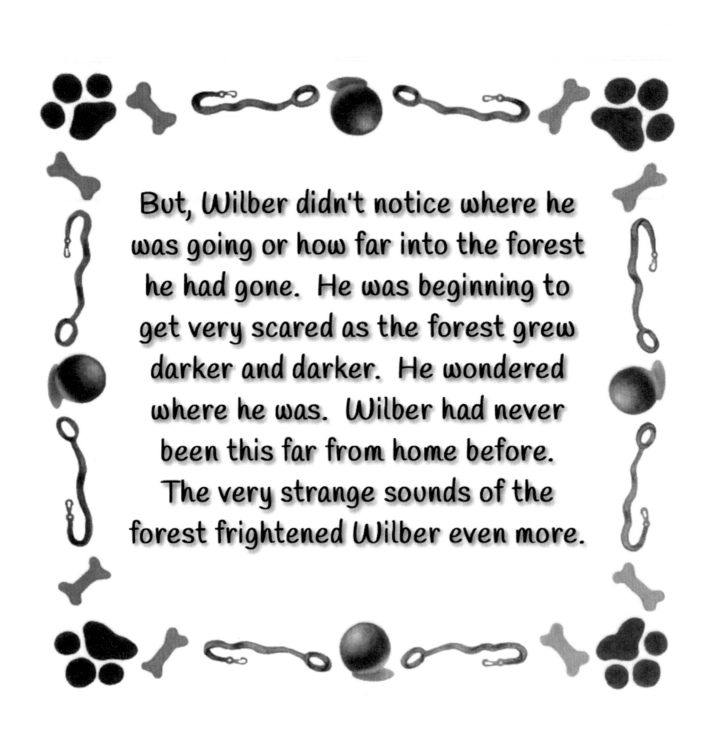

But, Wilber didn't notice where he was going or how far into the forest he had gone. He was beginning to get very scared as the forest grew darker and darker. He wondered where he was. Wilber had never been this far from home before. The very strange sounds of the forest frightened Wilber even more.

Wilber stopped and shivered with fright. His butterfly friends had flown off, and he lost sight of them, leaving him all alone in a very strange and dark place.

Now what was Wilber going to do? How was he going to find his way back home? Wilber was so worried, and it would be nightfall very soon.

He just kept hearing all of those terrible noises and awful sounds of the hoots and howls from strange and scary animals. He wasn't sure which direction he came from and he wasn't sure which way to go. He was lost!

Wilber suddenly started to think of his little boy. "Oliver will miss me he thought, "he will wonder where I am. I wish I wouldn't have gone so far from home."

A short time later he heard
the far off sound of something
coming in his direction.

He wasn't sure which direction the noises were
coming from. He wondered if he should hide.

Finally, Wilber saw
Oliver, with blonde
hair and big blue eyes.
He was holding a
bright red ball and
coming closer.

Wilber barked and wagged his tail, he was so happy. Then Oliver saw Wilber, and they ran to each other. Wilber was so excited that he knocked Oliver down and licked him all over. Oliver laughed and hugged Wilber. He was excited to see Wilber too.

"I thought I'd lost you, and I would never see you again," Oliver said. "I'm so glad you're ok Wilber. Let's go home. It's almost time for dinner." The two best friends stayed close together all the way home. Wilber said to himself, "I have learned my lesson. I will never go so far from home without my little boy again!"

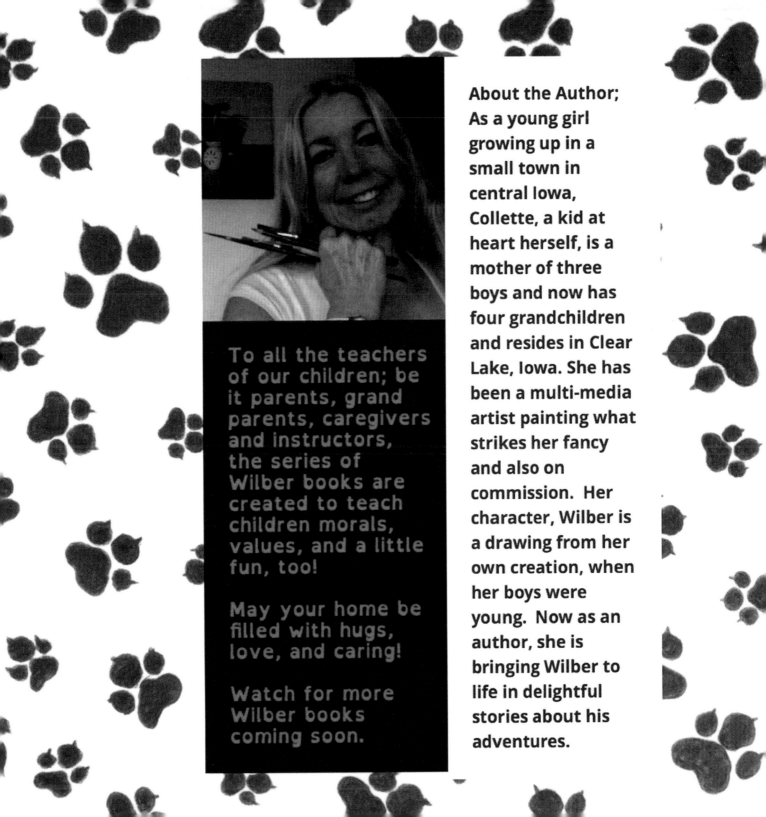

To all the teachers of our children; be it parents, grand parents, caregivers and instructors, the series of Wilber books are created to teach children morals, values, and a little fun, too!

May your home be filled with hugs, love, and caring!

Watch for more Wilber books coming soon.

About the Author;
As a young girl growing up in a small town in central Iowa, Collette, a kid at heart herself, is a mother of three boys and now has four grandchildren and resides in Clear Lake, Iowa. She has been a multi-media artist painting what strikes her fancy and also on commission. Her character, Wilber is a drawing from her own creation, when her boys were young. Now as an author, she is bringing Wilber to life in delightful stories about his adventures.